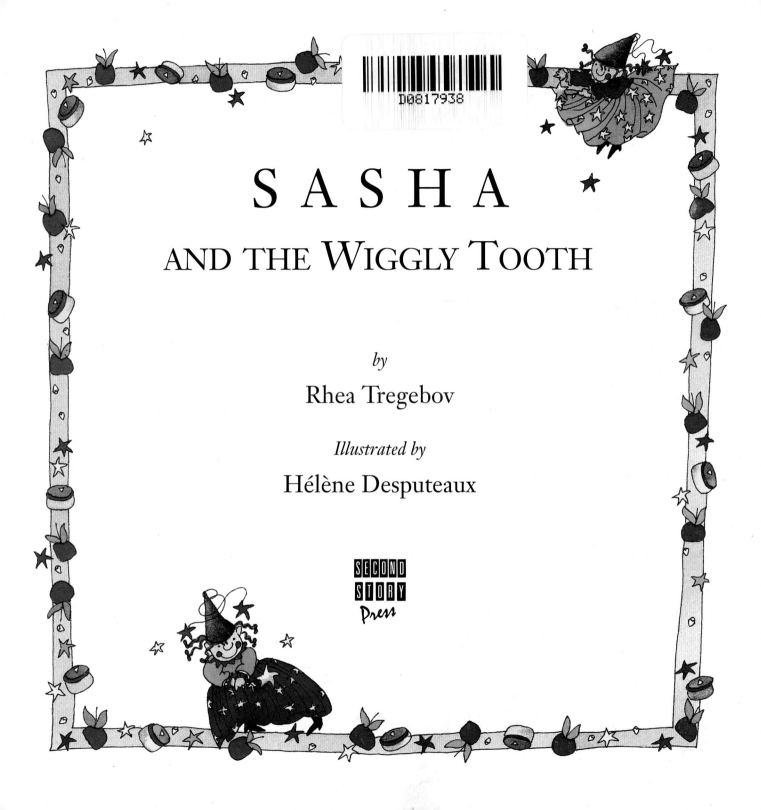

SASHA

AND THE WIGGLY TOOTH

by

Rhea Tregebov

Illustrated by

Hélène Desputeaux

SECOND STORY Press

All Sasha's friends were getting their big teeth. Talia had four. Daniella had two. And Tai had a hole at the bottom of his smile.

Sasha's teeth were baby teeth, but Sasha was no baby. He knew three times three was nine and could run faster than any of his friends.

"Don't worry, Sasha," said Talia. "We all get big teeth at different times."

"But does it hurt when they get wiggly?" asked Sasha.

"No. It sure feels weird, though."

"Mine came out when I bit an apple," said Tai. "I put it under my pillow and got money from the Tooth Fairy!"

"The Truth Fairy?" Sasha asked.

"The *Tooth* Fairy!" giggled Talia.

"Tai still believes in the Tooth Fairy," whispered Daniella. "She's just a story. She's not real, like Santa Claus."

The next morning, Sasha's front tooth in the middle felt different.

"Talia!" he shouted when he got to the playground. "My tooth is wiggly!"

Sasha told Tai and Daniella and his teacher and the library teacher and Tai's mom. He even phoned his grandmother.

"I feel *proud*," he told her, and smiled such a big smile that his grandmother almost saw it long distance.

Every day the tooth got wigglier, but Sasha stopped being excited. He wondered a bit and worried a little.

How would the tooth come out?

Would it hurt?

What would his new tooth be like?

What if the tooth fell out while he was playing baseball and he hit a grand slam and he lost the tooth between third base and home?

What would the Tooth Fairy do if his mother wanted to keep his tooth?

What if there *was* no Tooth Fairy?

One day the tooth was *so* wiggly it flipped back and forth like a doggy-door.

"I wish this tooth would just come OUT," Sasha told his friends.

"I could flick your wiggly tooth out with my super-strong thumbs!" said Daniella.

"I could buy you the biggest, stickiest toffee to chew," said Tai. "It would suck that tooth right out."

"We could turn you upside down and shake you," said Talia. "Your tooth would drop out then for sure!"

"Thank you," said Sasha, "but I'll wait till it falls out by itself."

At dinner that night Sasha's father looked at him — and then looked again.

"Sasha, where is your tooth?"

Sasha put the tip of his tongue where the tooth was supposed to be. His tongue went right through a space!

"It's gone!" he said, digging through his mashed potatoes with his fork.

"Where is it? WHERE IS MY TOOTH?"

"Maybe," said his father, "you swallowed it."

Sasha sat down very slowly. "Swallowed it? You mean it's lying at the bottom of my stomach? My tooth is supposed to be on my outside, not my inside. I think my tummy hurts."

"Baby teeth are pretty small," said his father. "I don't think it will give you a stomach-ache."

"But what about the Tooth Fairy?"

"That *is* a problem."

Sasha's father took out a round little box with a picture of a tooth on it. "The Tooth Fairy will look for your tooth in this box. What do you think we should do?"

"I know!" said Sasha. "We can put in a note instead of a tooth. *Then* the Tooth Fairy will understand."

Sasha ran to get a pencil.

"I don't really believe in the Tooth Fairy," said Sasha, and he chewed on his pencil a bit. "I'll print my note really small so it'll fit."

Dear Tooth Fairy,
    Are you real?
If you are, I hope this note is ok. I'd leave you my tooth but I swallowed it.

            Love, SaSha

Sasha lay awake a long long time.

The next morning, he looked in the tooth box under his pillow.

"Look," said Sasha, "the Tooth Fairy left me money and took my note!

"Hey! Maybe I could leave a note *every* night!"

"The Tooth Fairy will expect a tooth next time," said his father. "*This* time was special."

"*I* feel special," said Sasha.

And Sasha smiled such a big smile
that his grandmother almost
saw it long distance.